LOST AND FOUND

HarperCollins *Children's Books*

Once there was a boy...

and one cold autumn morning he found a penguin at his door.

The boy was not sure what this uninvited guest wanted, or where it was from...

but it had already outstayed its welcome.

For a problem like this, there was really only one thing to do...

find out where it came from and return it.

INVENTORY

SECTION 26 / ANIMALS

ITEM	DESCRIPTION	QTY
9"	ORANGE ~~BROWN~~ CAT 4 legs, 2 ears. Ran away monday FOUND	1
	MEDIUM SIZED SEAGULL Answers to 'BARNABY' usually grumpy	
	BEAVER Considers himself somewhat a DETECTIVE	
	RUBBER DUCKS last seen off	S

But no one, it seemed, was missing a penguin, so this was a problem that would not be solved so easily.

In fact, it was beginning
to look like a much bigger
problem than the boy
first realised.

PENGUIN

(Spheinisciphores)

...RGE FLIGHTLESS AQUATIC BIRD
...ally found in the Southern ...isphere
...ig 26). Not to be ... for
...tional Publishing ...
...hese birds ha...
...r backwards ... something
...hem.

... all Animals, are made of matter.

fig 1a
This is what a
penguin looks like.

HABITAT

PENGUINS COME FROM THE SOUTH POLE
otherwise known as ANTARCTICA.
The South Pole is a very cold place
that sits at the bottom of Planet
Earth. It finds itself at the opposite
end of the globe a... ...RTH POLE.
The South Pole is very very ... ...ay.

The
SOUTH
POLE

fig 2 a the South Pole

The boy decided that some proper thinking was called for, and after discovering that penguins come from the South Pole, he had an idea how to get the penguin home.

HOW TO
GET TO THE
SOUTH POLE

BY A. DUFAY

The boy asked a large ship to take them there.
But his voice was much too small to be heard. So, when things
aren't going your way, sometimes it's best to do them yourself.

The boy decided that together he and
the penguin would row to the South Pole.
They took the boy's rowboat out
of the cupboard, made a few
repairs and packed everything
they would need.

The boy worked out a plan for their journey, but he didn't once stop to think about why his visitor was there in the first place.

That night, he slept fitfully, for tomorrow he was going to try to cross the ocean to the other side of the earth.

In the morning, they pushed the rowboat out across the harbour and set off, prepared for anything the sea might do.

The boy rowed all day, stopping only for lunch,
and all seemed to be working out well.

But as the day gave way to night,
the small boat was a very long way from shore...

and they were about to find out exactly
what the sea could do when it wanted.

The wind howled, the rain poured in sideways
and the boy could not tell which way was which.

The waves rolled and grew and washed
the penguin's suitcase overboard.

When they thought the sea could not be any more angry,
waves came that were as big as mountains and it looked
certain their boat would be washed away.

After the storm had passed, they clung to the
side of their little boat with no hope left...

when an unlikely friend
rose from the deep and
put them back on their way.

And finally, after coming such a long way,
they saw it in the distance. The South Pole.

WELCOME
TO THE
SOUTH POLE

The boy's work was done.
They said an awkward goodbye.

Something didn't feel right at all, and the boy wasn't sure what it was. But then the penguin's lost suitcase floated up alongside the boat...

and everything became clear.
The penguin had not been
lost at all, but just lonely.
And perhaps he wasn't the only one.

The boy turned his boat around as fast
as possible and headed back to the South Pole.

He searched
and searched, but
he could not find
the penguin
anywhere.

He was sure he
would never see his
visitor again
and he set
off for
home.

After rowing towards home for some time he noticed something in the water ahead of him.

He rowed closer and closer
until he could see... the penguin.

And side by side, these friends from opposite sides of the ocean, rowed home together.

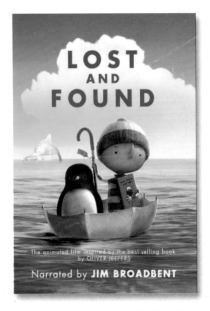

DVD AVAILABLE
FROM ALL GOOD RETAILERS

AWARD WINNING BOOKS BY
OLIVER JEFFERS

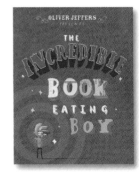

This film tie-in edition published as a paperback by HarperCollins Children's Books in 2009
1 3 5 7 9 10 8 6 4 2
ISBN: 978-0-00-731244-3
HarperCollins Children's Books is a division of HarperCollins Publishers Ltd.
Text and images based on Lost and Found Television Special © Contender Ltd/Studio AKA Ltd 2008
A CIP catalogue record for this title is available from the British Library.
Visit our website at: www.harpercollins.co.uk
Printed and bound in Italy

Lost and Found Television Special adapted by Philip Hunt and produced by Contender Ltd and Studio AKA